Reycraft Books
55 Fifth Avenue
New York, NY 10003

Reycraftbooks.com

© Text & Illustration by Hsu-Kung Liu
First Published in Complex Chinese © 2015 Hsiao Lu Publishing Co., Ltd.

Library of Congress Cataloging-in-Publication Data is available.

ISBN: 978-1-4788-6818-7

Printed in Guangzhou, China
4401/0919/CA21901489
10 9 8 7 6 5 4 3 2 1

First Edition Hardcover published by Reycraft Books 2019

Reycraft Books and Newmark Learning, LLC, support diversity and
the First Amendment, and celebrate the right to read.

The Orange Horse

HSU-KUNG LIU

Once upon a time, an orange
horse traveled to a faraway city.
He was looking for his
long-lost brother.

The only clue he had was **half a photograph** of an **orange horse**, just like him.

"There must be **another** orange horse out there with the other half of this photograph. If only I could find him," thought the horse.

One day, the orange horse had an idea.

"I could place an ad in the newspaper."

His ad said,

"If you are orange and are missing half an old photograph, please come and meet me."

The first to come see the orange

horse was an **orange house**.

And, of course, their pictures did

not match at all.

"My brother should be a **good runner**,

like I am," the orange horse thought.

And so, he changed his ad to,

"If you are orange, have half
an old photograph, and can run
fast, please come and meet me."

An **orange race car** was the next to come see the orange horse. But, of course, their pictures did **not** match.

"My brother should have a **black mane** and a **black tail**," the orange horse told himself. So he added more words to his ad,

"If you are orange, have half an old photograph, run fast, and have a black mane and a black tail, please come and meet me."

This time, an **orange lion** answered the ad.

He was orange and he ran fast.

He also had a black mane and a black tail.

However, his photograph did **not** match

the orange horse's.

The orange horse felt very tired and sad.

"I will never find my **missing brother**,"

thought the orange horse, with a sigh.

One day, while he was visiting an art gallery, the orange horse met a **brown horse**.

The brown horse came from far away and had visited many lands on his way to the city where the orange horse lived. He told the orange horse lots of interesting things about the places he had been and the people he had met. The orange horse felt a special kind of bond with this brown horse.

He had never **felt so happy** before.

The whole city glowed bright, and life
seemed full of hope and happiness.

Sometimes, the **two horses** ran together.

Sometimes, they ate together. And they always

had so much to talk about.

"How **wonderful** it would be if the brown horse

were my brother!" thought the orange horse.

One night, the brown horse mentioned that he too had a **long-lost brother** . . . and half an old photograph.

The orange horse felt a tiny
glimmer of **hope**.

But no, their
half-photographs
were **not** a match.

The orange horse felt sad and disappointed.

If only the half-photos did not exist!

Then there would still be hope that they

were **real brothers**.

The brown horse was **angry** and **upset**. With a pair of scissors, he started trimming the two half-photographs.

Then he stuck the two halves together.

"Don't cry," he told the orange horse.

"See? From now on, we are **brothers.**"

From then on, despite their difference in color, the **orange horse** and the **brown horse** have been the best friends — and brothers — ever.

HSU-KUNG LIU

 lives and works in
Taipei, Taiwan.
He really likes
nature and people.
His typical day includes drawing
and writing, and he has taught
art at several schools. He has won
many awards, including the Hsin-
Yi Children's Literature Award, and
was twice featured at the Bologna
International Children's Book Fair
Illustrators Exhibition.